PRETTY STAR
THE PONY
AND OTHER STORIES

Pretty Star the Pony

and Other Stories

by
ENID BLYTON

Illustrated by
Sally Gregory

AWARD PUBLICATIONS

ISBN 0-86163-406-3

Text copyright © Darrell Waters Limited
Illustrations copyright © 1989 Award Publications Limited

Enid Blyton's signature is a trademark of Darrell Waters Limited

This edition entitled *Pretty-Star the Pony and Other Stories*
First published 1989
4th impression 1992

Published by Award Publications Limited,
Spring House, Spring Place, Kentish Town, London NW5 3BH

Printed in Hungary

CONTENTS

6

Boody the Great Goblin

Once upon a time there was a very clever goblin called Boody. He had six hundred magic books, and he knew more spells than any goblin in the land. But there was one spell he wanted to know which he couldn't seem to find out.

'How can I make old people young?' he wondered. 'How can I make old eyes shine again, and bent limbs straight? If only I knew that, I should make my fortune!'

He read his magic books every day, and he asked every witch and wizard he knew if they could help him. But no one could.

Then one day he decided to try to make a spell that would do what he wanted. So he got together six fresh violets, picked at sunrise, four hairs from a lamb's tail, a smile from a month-old baby, a kitten's whisker, and many other queer things. He put them all together into a big blue pot and made a fire of young twigs on the hillside. Every morning at break of day he stirred the mixture seven times and chanted magic words.

Well, when the spell was made he gave a little sip to Hoity-Toity, his old black cat. Imagine his delight when Hoity became as frolicsome as a kitten, and was just like he used to be ten years back.

'Now I have found the right spell!' cried Boody the goblin. 'Now I shall make my fortune!'

The next day and the next he spent in writing all about how he had found his famous spell, and what he had put into it. But, alas, when the third day came Hoity-Toity the cat was no longer young and sprightly. He looked as old as ever, and wouldn't even mew when

Boody said 'Good morning!' to him.

'Oh, dear, there's something wrong with that spell after all!' said Boody in dismay. 'I have left out something important – now what can it be?'

He thought and thought, and looked up all his magic books – then suddenly he came across just the thing he wanted.

He found that the golden hairs of a seventeen-year-old princess had a great power in spells of the sort he was making. Boody worked excitedly, trying to find how many he would need. At last he discovered it.

'If I stir into my mixture a golden hair freshly plucked from the head of a seventeen-year-old princess, every morning for a month, I shall make the spell quite perfect!' cried Boody. 'Oh, this is splendid!'

But after a while he began to frown. Where ever could he get twenty-eight golden hairs, and what princess would give them to him?

He didn't waste much time in finding

out. He called his little servant, Peepo, to him, and bade him go swiftly on bat's wings to every princess in the world, and see if he could find one aged seventeen who had golden hair.

In an hour's time, Peepo came back.

'Master,' he said, bowing low, 'I have visited every court in the world. There are five princesses aged seventeen, and three of these have golden hair.'

'Good!' said Boody, 'we have three to choose from, then.'

'Not so, Master,' said Peepo. 'One of the princesses will be eighteen tomorrow, and another is dyeing her hair black to please the king she is going to marry.'

'Oh my!' groaned Boody. 'Well, what about the third?'

'She is just seventeen,' said Peepo, 'and her hair is like the sunshine itself. But, Master, you will never get her father, the king, to consent to the princess giving you any of her golden hairs, for he has banished all the goblins from his kingdom, and will not let

one live there, no matter how harmless he is. A goblin did him a bad turn once in his youth, and this is his revenge.'

Boody sat thinking. It was too bad that he could not get just the last thing he wanted. He knew that it was of no use going to ask the king's consent – and there was another thing that he had not told Peepo. The princess whose hairs he used would lose all her beauty at the end of a month, and appear to be an old, old woman.

The cunning little goblin would not give up his plans. He meant to get those golden hairs somehow. He lay awake all night long, and when day dawned he had made up his mind what to do. He would capture the princess and bring her to his cave! Then every morning he would pluck a golden hair from her head, and thus he would be able to complete his spell.

The next day he set out. He was invisible, for around his shoulders was a wide cape made from witches' shadows. Anyone wearing such a

mantle could be seen by neither man, woman nor child. Only animals could see him, and they shrank back in fear.

At noon he reached the palace where Princess Goldie dwelt. She was in her room alone, threading some blue beads to wear that evening. Boody ran unseen up the stairs, entered the room of the princess, and flung his wide cloak round her. In a moment she was invisible! She screamed in fright, and her maidens came running in at once.

'Help me! Help me!' cried the princess. But though the maidens looked here and there, they could see nothing. Boody carried the princess down the stairs, and the footmen there started in astonishment to hear their princess's voice calling to them, though they could see no one.

'It's a horrid little goblin who's taking me away!' cried Goldie. 'Oh, come and save me!'

The king came rushing out when he heard his daughter's voice, and all the soldiers ran here and there. But nobody

could do anything, for the princess and Boody were invisible.

In four hours Princess Goldie was safely in the goblin's cave. He rolled a great stone over the entrance, and then carried her down the long winding passage to his rocky home. Peepo was there, and stared in amazement to see the lovely princess in his master's arms.

'I have got her,' said Boody in delight. 'It will be your task, Peepo, to look after her, and see that she does not escape. Every morning I will take a golden hair, and then, in a month's time, my marvellous spell will be finished.'

Goldie was put in a little underground room with a bed and a chair. She was frightened and miserable, and she hated the ugly little goblin. She was so tired that she fell asleep, and did not wake until dawn the next day. Just as she awoke, the goblin came in.

'Give me a hair from your head,' he said.

'No, I won't,' said Goldie. 'You shan't have a single one, you horrid little man. How dare you take me away from my palace? When my father knows, he will come and rescue me, and then you will be punished.'

Now never in all his long life had Boody been spoken to like that, and he was very angry.

He snatched a hair from Goldie's shining head, and pulled it out.

'There!' he said, 'I've got it! And every morning for a month you will have to give me one. At the end of that time you will lose your youth and beauty, and that will punish you for your rudeness to me, Boody the Great Goblin!'

'Great fiddlesticks!' cried the princess, and she slapped the goblin's face.

How angry Boody was! He ran out of the little room in a rage, longing to spank the princess, but not daring to stop in case he missed the dawn.

As soon as he had gone the princess began to cry. She tried the door, but it was fast bolted. She kicked at it, and hammered on it with her fists, but she could not open it. Then at last she heard the bolts being slipped out, and

she saw Peepo coming in.

When he saw the tears on the face of the lovely princess, he stopped in dismay.

'Don't cry, Princess Goldie,' he said. 'You have only got to be here a month.

Nothing will happen to you, and you will be taken back quite safely to your palace.'

'Something *will* happen to me!' sobbed the princess. 'That horrid goblin told me that at the end of the month I shall lose all my youth and beauty!'

Peepo stared in horror. What! Would this lovely maiden become old and ugly just because his master wanted to use her hair for his spells? Peepo's heart was full of sadness. He had never seen such a beautiful maid before, and he could not bear to think that she should be unhappy.

Goldie saw his sorrowful face, and she ran to him. She put her arms

round his neck, and spoke beseech-
ingly to him.

'Please, please help me to get away,'
she said. 'You have such a kind face,
and I am so unhappy.'

Peepo went red with delight to feel
Goldie's arms round his neck. No one
had ever hugged him before or been
kind to him. As long as he could remember he had been servant to Boody,
and had done his bidding. The goblin
had been rough and unkind to him, and
Peepo had often been miserable.

'I would like to help you, princess,' he
said in a whisper, 'but I am so afraid of
Boody the goblin. If he finds out that I
want to help you, he would turn me into
a toad and put me in the middle of a
tree for a hundred years. He would
really.'

'Well, couldn't you go and find someone who isn't afraid of Boody, and could
come and rescue me?' asked Goldie. 'Oh
please do go, Peepo, and tell someone
where I am.'

'All right,' said Peepo, beginning to

tremble when he thought of Boody's anger when he found out. 'I'll go tonight when Boody is asleep.'

So that night when the goblin was snoring away in his hard bed, Peepo slipped out into the starlight. Where should he go, and whom should he tell?

He had only a little while, for dawn came early, and the goblin was always awake then.

He ran down the hillside and came to the lane at the bottom. Up it he ran and then sped on until he came to a little cottage. Here dwelt an old man and his wife, with their young son.

Peepo rattled at the shutters and called softly. The old man awoke and sent his son to see what was the matter.

The boy was astonished to find a tiny dwarf under the window.

'What do you want?' he asked.

'I come with a message from the Princess Goldie,' whispered Peepo, fearful lest the bats should hear and tell the goblin about him. 'She is shut up in one of Boody the Great Goblin's caves, and every day for a month he is going to take one of her golden hairs for a new spell of his. At the end of that time she will lose all her youth and beauty, so she must be rescued quickly indeed!'

The boy listened in surprise. Then suddenly he reached out his hand and grabbed hold of Peepo's shoulder. He dragged him through the window and looked at him by the light of his candle.

'Why don't you rescue her yourself,' he asked.

'I daren't,' said Peepo. 'The goblin, my master, is too powerful. But please let me go now – I must be home by dawn or the goblin will see I have been out and will punish me.'

But the boy would not let him go. He kept him there, asking question after question till Peepo was full of terror lest he should be out too late to get back unseen.

At last the boy lifted him out of the window again, and Peepo ran for his life. Alas for the little servant! Boody was just coming out of the cave as Peepo came in. He saw by the little dwarf's face that he had been betraying him, and he pounced on him.

In an instant Peepo was turned into a toad, and Boody shut him up in a tree for a hundred years. Then he went to the princess, took one of her golden hairs, and told her what he had done to Peepo.

'That is *your* fault,' he said to the weeping maiden. 'Do not hope that you will be rescued. I have placed a magic circle outside your door, and whoever steps into it will dissolve at once into smoke!'

He left the frightened princess and went up to the top of the hill with her golden hair. Goldie was in despair. She felt quite certain that no one could save her, and all day long she wept her pretty eyes out.

Now the boy who had listened to Peepo was a very sharp lad. He was determined to find out if the story that the little dwarf had told was true. Without being seen by Peepo, he followed him as he ran back to the cave. He saw Boody catch him, and watched in horror as the poor little servant was turned into a toad.

The lad ran off as soon as he could, and made up his mind to fetch help. So that day he walked across the hills to where a large palace stood. In it dwelt the chancellor of that land, a very powerful man. The boy saw him, and told his story.

'I will ride straight to the king,' said the chancellor. 'I will ask him if he has heard of any princess being missing from the countries round about. If your tale is true, you shall be well rewarded for your trouble.'

The chancellor started off with his swiftest horses. He soon arrived at the king's palace, and told him what he had heard. No sooner had he finished than a courier was seen riding at top speed into the courtyard.

'Perhaps this messenger bears the news!' said the king. Sure enough, he did! He came with a letter from the king of a neighbouring country.

'My daughter, Princess Goldie, has been stolen by a goblin,' said the letter. 'There are goblins in your kingdom. I pray you to seek out every one and see if my daughter is hidden anywhere in your land.'

Now the king's son, Prince Merry, had been listening to all that had been said. He was young and handsome, brave and daring. He knew Princess Goldie, and thought her the sweetest little maiden in the world. When he heard that the goblin had taken her away, he leapt to his feet and drew his sword.

'I shall go and find her!' he cried.

'Sit down, Merry,' said the king, 'you are too young – besides, these goblins are very powerful. You might find yourself turned into a snail or a spider.'

But Merry would not listen. He strode out of the palace and, leaping on his swiftest horse, he rode to the cot-

tage where the little boy lived who had heard the dwarf's tale the night before. He bade the child get up behind him, and then he rode to where the nearby mountains raised their heads to the sky.

'This is where the goblins live,' said the boy. 'I have often seen them running about. And do you see that highest hill, Your Highness? It is there that every morning a goblin goes to stir something in a great bowl, for I have often lain on the hill opposite and watched him.'

Merry rode to the hill the boy pointed to, and the lad showed him where he had seen the dwarf changed into a toad the night before. Merry looked closely at the cave opening, and decided that it would be folly to try and force an entrance that way. The goblin would hear him easily, and before he knew what was happening he would be bewitched in some way.

He rode round to the back of the hill, and dismounted. He looked carefully at the hillside, and scraped the earth with his foot. It was very sandy and came away easily.

'I have an idea,' he said to the lad. 'I believe I could dig through this hill, and come into the goblin's cave from the back. But how I wish I could think of some way by which I might put him off his guard!'

'Your Highness,' said the boy, red with excitement, 'I know. The goblin has no servants now – shall I go and offer myself as one? If he took me, I could find out exactly where the princess is and let you know. I could try and think of some way, too, that would make him keep such a sharp look-out in front of his hill that he would quite neglect the other side of it!'

'Brave boy!' said the prince. 'Go at once and try your luck. Come back to me here tonight, and tell me what happens.'

The boy went. The goblin saw him and was pleased to be able to get another servant so quickly, for few people cared to work for goblins. He would not let the lad go into the princess's room, but the boy soon found out exactly where it was.

'Keep a good look-out,' said the goblin. 'See that no stranger comes peering round here, and tell me at once if you see anyone.'

The boy grinned to himself. He meant to give the goblin so many false alarms that he would have too much work to do in watching the front of his cave to bother about the back of the hill.

So all day long he rushed in and out to the goblin crying out this, that and the other, so that Boody was in such a fright he thought only of the front entrance to his cave. If so much as a tiny pebble fell down the hill the lad would tear in, shouting, 'Master! Master! There is a rumbling, roaring sound! Can it be a wizard?'

When night came the boy stole out to see the prince. Merry had begun digging into the hill, and the boy was able

to tell him about how far he would have to go before he came to the deep cave where lay the golden-haired princess. All through the night the prince dug hard. He slept the next day, but when night came he again began to dig. Soon he had made quite a long tunnel in the hill, and he thought he must be coming near to where the cave of the princess was.

Then a dreadful thing happened. As he tunnelled a rock fell from the roof of the passage he had made, and struck him on the head. He fell in a faint, and lay on the ground until the boy came creeping out for his nightly talk. He found the prince lying there, and hastily dragged him out on the hillside where the air was clean and cool.

He saw that Merry was badly hurt, so he fetched a cottager and bade him carry the prince to his home and tend him. This the man was glad to do, for he saw that the young man was of royal rank.

For three weeks Merry lay ill. Then

he got back his strength, and when the lad came to see him, he dressed and went out with him.

'Oh, Your Highness! Are you strong enough to go on with the digging?' asked the boy. 'There are only two nights left before Boody the goblin takes the twenty-eighth hair from the head of the princess. Then she will lose all her youth and beauty, and great misery will be her lot.'

'I shall be in time!' said the prince. He took off his coat and began to go on with his tunnelling. All night long he worked furiously. Then, just before dawn, he knew he must be somewhere near the cave – for he heard a harsh voice speaking nearby.

'One more morning, Princess Goldie – and my spell will be finished!'

He heard the princess weeping, and put his hand on his sword in rage to think that such a horrid little goblin should have power over Goldie.

He did not dare to dig any farther that day, in case the goblin should hear him. But when night came he set carefully to work.

Goldie did not sleep that night. She was so afraid of the morning, and what it would bring her. As she lay on her bed, weeping, she heard a curious scraping noise. What could it be?

She sat up and listened. Was it a mouse? A rat? Or perhaps a rabbit? No, it could not be any of those, for it was too loud. Oh, was it someone coming to save her?

She watched the wall of the cave from behind which the noise seemed to come. It grew louder. Whatever was behind it was getting nearer. Goldie's heart beat fast. She lighted her candle, and watched to see what was going to happen.

Suddenly the prince put his pick right through the wall of the cave. A great hole appeared, and he put his head through.

'Goldie!' he said. 'Oh, you poor little princess! I am Prince Merry, and I have come to save you!'

'Sh! Sh!' said Goldie. 'You are only just in time. The goblin may be here at any moment. Have I got time to go with you?'

But even as she spoke the goblin was coming to the cave to pluck the twenty-eighth golden hair from her head. Prince Merry heard him, and leapt behind the great door that shut up the entrance to the underground room. Boody opened it, and at once the prince sprang at him.

'Ha!' he cried. 'I have you, you wicked old goblin!'

Boody gave a scream, and dropped on his knees. He was terrified of the gleaming sword that the prince was holding above his head.

'Mercy! Mercy!' he cried.

'Not an ounce of mercy shall I show you!' said the prince, sternly. 'You shall die!'

'Oh wait a minute!' cried Goldie, suddenly remembering the little servant Peepo who had been turned into a toad for trying to help her. 'Tell him to change Peepo back into his right shape again.'

The prince took firm hold of Boody's collar and made him lead the way up the winding passages to the entrance of his cave. Then he made him get the toad from the tree and change it back into Peepo. How glad the little servant was! He ran to the prince and kissed his feet.

'Now for your punishment!' said Merry to the trembling goblin. He raised his bright sword – but suddenly there was a tremendous BANG! And Boody had vanished! Everyone gaped in astonishment – but no matter where they looked, the goblin was not there!

'He's gone for ever,' said Peepo. 'He'll never come back. Hurrah! Now let's go

and be happy!'

Off they all went to the king's palace, taking the boy with them, too, for he had helped greatly in the rescue. He was made a nobleman, and Peepo the dwarf became the prince's own servant, which made him very proud indeed.

As for the prince and princess you can guess what happened to *them*. They were married to each other and lived happily ever after.

Pretty-Star the Pony

I am a little black pony, and my name is Pretty-Star because I have a pretty white star right in the middle of my forehead.

I used to live in Farmer White's field, and eat the sweet grass there. I didn't like Farmer White, for he was a rough man with a loud voice that made me jump with fright. When he rode me I felt as if my back was going to give way, for he was so heavy. He gave me the whip, too, and that is enough to break any willing pony's heart, for I never needed it.

A little girl called Mary used to come and see me every day. She lived in a house near to Farmer White's and went to school on her bicycle every morning. On her way there and back she would stop and speak to me. Sometimes she brought me lumps of sugar, or an apple.

'I wish you were *my* pony,' she would say. 'I would love to have you for my very own. I would ride you to school every day, and look after you well, dear little Pretty-Star. When my birthday comes I am going to ask my Daddy to buy you for me.'

One day her bicycle had a puncture, so she came and asked Farmer White if he would lend me to her to ride to school on. He said yes, so she put my saddle and bridle on, and jumped up on my back. How proud I was to carry her! I neighed gladly, and trotted along carefully. She was as light as a feather, and didn't pull at my mouth a bit. She talked to me all the way, and though I couldn't answer her in her own language, I loved to hear her voice.

She gave me an apple and tied me up to the school gate in the shade of a tree, just within reach of some nice juicy grass. There I waited patiently until she came out to go home again.

'Oh, Pretty-Star, I *wish* you were my very own pony,' she said, when she let me loose in Farmer White's field again. 'I am sure we should love each other dearly.'

When her birthday came she brought her father to see me.

'Daddy, will you give me this little black pony for my birthday?' she asked.

'I want him more than anything else in the world.'

'But what would you do with him?' asked her father. 'You've got your bicycle to ride to school on. You'd soon get tired of having to look after a real live pony. It's not like a bicycle, you know, Mary. You couldn't just put him in a shed and leave him there till you wanted him. He would have to be fed,

48

and groomed carefully.'

'Yes, Daddy,' said Mary. 'I know just how to groom him, and I could take care of him much better than Farmer White does, really I could. He doesn't care a bit for him.'

I nuzzled my nose into Mary's hand, and looked at her father pleadingly, for I wanted to belong to Mary. But the big man shook his head.

'No,' he said. 'I must disappoint you, Mary. The pony is quite a nice little thing, but he is not worth the price Farmer White is asking. I'll buy you a big doll instead.'

Mary didn't say any more, but she gave me a hug and a kiss, and I knew better than her father how sad she was not to have me for her own.

Mary got her big doll, but she wouldn't play with it. She was the sort of person who likes real live pets that love her back when she loves them. She came to see me every day, and I whinnied a welcome, and ran to meet her.

One day she came to the nearby river to fish with her big boy cousin. I stood as near to them as I could, but I couldn't get very near because of a high hedge in between. Mary waved to me when she saw my head over the hedge, and I whinnied back.

I watched them all the morning. They didn't catch any fish, and the big boy was impatient.

'Let's climb up on this rock where there's a deep, quiet pool beneath,' he said. 'I'm sure there are plenty of fish there, Mary.'

'We must be careful then,' said Mary.

'It is dangerous to climb up there, my Daddy says.'

I knew it was, too, and I watched them anxiously. They had just reached the top of the rock when Mary slipped. She clutched at the boy and missed him. Then she fell right over the rock and I heard her fall *splash!* into the deep pool below.

'Mary, Mary!' called the boy. 'Can you swim?'

I knew she wasn't able to, but of course I couldn't tell him that. I was so anxious that I didn't know what to do. I couldn't get out of my field, for the gate was shut, and I ran whinnying round and round and round, thinking of Mary

52

in the water. I hoped the boy would dive in and rescue her, but he didn't.

I suddenly saw him start running off towards the house where Mary lived. He was calling 'Help! Help! Mary is in the water!' as he ran.

Well, I knew that the little girl would drown if no one rescued her soon, and I was almost mad with grief. I decided to get to the river if I only could. So I ran backwards a few paces, then galloped full tilt at the high hedge. Over I went, with my hoofs just touching the top. I have never jumped so high before, and I don't suppose I ever shall again.

Once over the hedge I raced down to the river. I looked into the water, and soon saw where Mary was. She was holding on to a broken bough of a tree that dipped down to the river, and I knew that it would soon break off altogether, and then my little friend would drown.

I jumped straight into the river myself, and began to swim towards Mary.

I had nearly got to her when the bough broke right off, and the little girl went under the water. She came up spluttering and gasping – but she saw me.

'Help me, Pretty-Star!' she cried – then down she went again.

In a trice I was up to her. I plucked hold of her wet clothes with my strong teeth, and pulled her up. She came up spluttering again, and caught hold of my neck.

'Hold on tightly,' I said in my horse language that she understood so well. So she held on whilst I turned myself carefully round in the water, and began to swim for the shallow bank. The current was against me, and it was very difficult. I am only a little pony, and Mary seemed very heavy, with all her wet clothes dragging her down. I began to gasp and pant myself, and I felt as if my heart was bursting in two.

Then I saw some people running towards the river. There was the boy and Mary's father and Mother, and the gardener, too, carrying a rope. They all

ran to the bank, and looked down on Mary and me.

'The pony's got her! He must have jumped right over the hedge!' cried Mary's father in amazement.

'Oh, the brave little pony!' cried Mary's mother, with tears streaming down her cheeks.

Just at that moment I reached the bank, and stumbled out of the water. I was so exhausted that I had to lie down in the mud. Mary's father picked her up and fondled her, and her mother cried tears all over her.

'I'm all right, Daddy,' said Mary. 'But just look at that poor little tired pony. I'm sure he must nearly have burst his heart in two, swimming against the river like that.'

Fancy her knowing that! That just shows how she loved me. Of course, I soon felt better, then, dear me, the petting I had! It was wonderful!

Nobody could make enough of me. I had sugar and apples, and everyone stroked my nose and patted me. It was lovely.

But the nicest reward of all was still to come.

'Mary, we'll take the pony back to Farmer White now,' said her father. 'And if he's still willing to sell him, you shall have him. He deserves to belong to you, for I never saw such a plucky little creature in my life!'

Pretty-Star the Pony

Farmer White said he was quite willing to sell me. So Mary's father paid for me that same day, and Mary rode on my back to her home. I was her very own pony at last!

And now I am as happy as the day is long, for I take Mary to and from school every day, and we always go for a long ride together in the evenings. On Saturdays we go out all day long together, and on Sundays I take her to church. Don't you think I am a very lucky little pony?

In Nursery-Rhyme Land

Betty and John had a lovely wallpaper in their playroom. It showed all the nursery-rhyme folk going about their work. There were Jack and Jill going up the hill, Tommy Tucker singing for his supper, Little Bo Peep looking for her sheep, and many, many others.

Betty and John were never tired of looking at their wallpaper. There were trees and hills on it, and little round ponds with ducks. There were funny houses, and there was Noah's ark floating on a river, with Mr and Mrs Noah looking out of the window. A great many of the animals were peeping out of the top, and they all looked very happy. It really was a *lovely* wallpaper.

'Don't you wish we could visit the land on our wallpaper?' asked Betty one day. 'It does look so exciting, and we should be able to meet so many nursery-rhyme folk!'

John wished they could, too, but he felt certain that they never would. Things like that never seemed to happen to people.

But one evening, as they were sitting by the fire reading a book, John happened to look up at the wallpaper – and he saw a very strange thing.

All the people on it were moving! Jack and Jill were really walking up the hill, Noah's ark was really floating along the river and Little Jack Horner was really eating his pie!

'I must be dreaming!' said John, in the greatest surprise. 'I say, Betty! Look at the wallpaper! Does it seem different to you?'

Betty looked, and then she jumped to her feet in astonishment.

'Why, all the people are alive!' she cried. 'Oh, John! Let's call Mummy!'

'No, don't let's,' said John. 'The wall-paper would go quite ordinary again as soon as she came in. I know it would. Let's go nearer and look at it. Oh, Betty! Isn't it peculiar!'

The two children ran close to the paper, and looked at it. There was no doubt that everyone on it was moving.

'It doesn't look like a paper now,' said Betty. 'It looks like real land, only very far away. Oh, John, John! It's suddenly getting bigger!'

John caught hold of Betty's hand, and held it tight. Yes, everything in the paper was getting very large. Whatever was going to happen?

The two children stood quite still and stared hard. In front of them was a little house, and this seemed to be getting nearly as big as a real house.

Soon it was so big that the children couldn't see anything else at all. It hid everything.

'John! It's not a paper house, it's *real*!' said Betty. 'Look, the chimney's smoking! Something very strange has

happened. Oh, dear, it's rather frightening – but isn't it *exciting*!'

'Where's the playroom?' said John, looking behind him. 'Why, Betty, it's gone! We're standing in the garden of the little house! It must be magic, really it must!'

Sure enough the playroom was gone. The children were standing on a tiny path in front of the little house they had so often seen on their wallpaper. They had wondered who lived there, for the door was shut, and there was no one looking out of the window.

'Well, we've often wanted an adventure, and now we've got one!' said John. 'Let's enjoy it, Betty!'

The sun was shining all around them, which was very strange, because it had been evening time in the playroom. It seemed about midday, and was very hot.

'We can't stand on this garden path all day,' said John. 'What shall we do, Betty?'

Just as he said that the door of the

cottage opened, and out came a little girl with a bowl of curds and whey in her hands.

'It's Little Miss Muffet!' said John, in excitement. 'Now we know who lives in this cottage, Betty.'

'Good morning,' said Little Miss Muffet. 'What are you doing on my garden path? Did you want to see me?'

'No,' said John. 'We just found ourselves here. Please excuse us. We are very glad to see you.'

'That's nice of you,' said Miss Muffet. 'Come with me. I'll show you a dear little tuffet of grass that I always sit on every day to eat my curds and whey.'

She ran down the path and out of the gate. The two children followed her. She took them to a little wood, and there, under the trees, was a small grassy seat, just high enough for a little girl to sit on. Miss Muffet sat down, and smiled at Betty and John.

'Would you like to sit on it just for once?' she asked Betty. Betty said yes, she would love to. So down she sat, thinking what a dear little tuffet it was.

But suddenly John began to shout and scream.

'Get up, Betty! Quick, get up! Here's the spider! Oh quick! It's the biggest I've ever seen!'

Betty jumped up in a dreadful hurry. Sure enough, letting itself down from a tree just over Betty's head, was a spider nearly as big as Betty herself! Miss Muffet screamed and ran away, leaving her curds and whey beside the tuffet. Betty ran too, and John caught hold of her hand and ran with her.

When they had run a long way, they turned and looked back. The spider was sitting on the tuffet, eating Miss Muffet's curds and whey!

'Just fancy that!' cried John. 'He does that every day, I expect. If I were Miss Muffet I wouldn't go and sit on that tuffet any more, would you, Betty?'

'No,' said Betty, with a shiver, for she didn't very much like spiders. 'Miss Muffet's gone, John. I expect she went back to her little house. Come on, let's go and find someone else.'

They went on down a little winding lane. Soon they came to a small boy sitting in a corner of a field, eating a big pie. He had very bad manners, for instead of using a spoon, he put in his thumb and finger, and pulled the plums out with them.

'It's Little Jack Horner!' whispered Betty.

'What a good boy am I!' said Jack Horner, popping a great big plum into his mouth. 'Hello, you two! Where are you going?'

'We don't know,' said John. 'We're just wandering about.'

'Oh, well, mind you don't get caught by the Old Woman Who Lives in a Shoe,' said Jack Horner, taking out another plum, and popping it into his mouth. 'She's lost some of her children, and she's out looking for them. If she catches you you'll have a very bad time. She feeds them on broth without any bread, and whips them all soundly and

sends them to bed.'

'Good gracious!' said John, in alarm. 'Do you really think she would try and catch us, Jack?'

'Rather!' said Jack. 'She tried to get me yesterday, but I got the Cow with the Crumpled Horn to frighten her off. The old cow is a great friend of mine, you know. She lives in this field. Look, there she is.'

John and Betty looked. They saw a fat brown cow grazing nearby. One of her horns was all crumpled. She looked at them with her great eyes, and then went on grazing.

'Hi! Look out! There's the Old Woman!' Jack Horner suddenly cried. John and Betty looked round quickly. They saw an old woman coming up the lane, carrying in her hand the birch with which she whipped her children.

John caught hold of Betty's hand, and ran for his life. The Old Woman saw them, and at once began to run after them.

'Come here, you naughty children!'

she cried. 'I've been looking for you everywhere. Come back to the shoe at once.'

Betty and John tore down the lane. They turned the corner, and came to a little cottage. The front door was open, so without thinking they ran into it, shut the door, and then peeped out of the window. The Old Woman soon

came by. She stopped at the gate and looked all about. John and Betty trembled – but she didn't come in. Instead she stood at the gate as if she was waiting for someone.

Soon that someone came. It was a little girl carrying a doll, and she came dancing to the gate and opened it. Then the Old Woman stretched out her hand and took hold of her shoulder.

'You're one of my lost children!' she said, in a very cross voice.

'Indeed I'm not!' said the little girl, tossing her head. 'I'm Mary, Mary, Quite Contrary, and this is my house and garden. Take your hand off me, Old Woman, and go away!'

'You rude little girl!' said the Old Woman. 'It will do you good to come and live in my shoe for a while. You shall come with me and learn manners!'

Mary began to cry, but it was no good. Off she had to go with the Old Woman. Betty and John looked on in dismay, very glad to think they had not been caught too.

'This must be Mary Quite Contrary's garden,' said John. 'Look, there are the silver bells hung on sticks, and all the beds are edged with cockle-shells. But what are those dolls sitting out there?'

'Why, those are the pretty maids all in row!' said Betty. 'Don't you remember the nursery rhyme, John?'

'Oh, yes,' said John. 'Well, come on, Betty. We'd better leave here, and go on again. What an adventure this is!'

'I do hope we don't meet that horrid Old Woman again!' said Betty. 'I'd like to see Noah's Ark, wouldn't you, John?'

'Yes,' said John. 'Let's ask the way to the river.'

So when they met Little Bo Peep looking for her sheep, they asked her the way, and she told them.

'You don't happen to have seen my sheep, do you?' she asked. 'I keep losing them, the naughty things.'

'No, we haven't seen any sheep at all,' said John. 'Only the Cow with a Crumpled Horn.'

On they went again, and soon came to the river. And there, floating on the water, was Noah's ark. Mr and Mrs Noah were looking out of the window, and all the animals were peeping out of the top, just as they had done in the wallpaper. But now they were very big, and the ark was like a great house.

'Good morning!' cried Mr and Mrs Noah. 'Do come in and see us! We'll send the hippo over to you, and you can climb on his back. Then he will carry you across.'

All the animals began to bellow and roar, howl and bark, and Betty and John felt a bit frightened.

'I don't think we will, thank you,' said John. 'The animals don't seem to want us very much.'

'Bless you, that's only their way of saying 'Do come!' said Mrs Noah. '*They* won't hurt you.'

But the lion looked rather fierce, and John and Betty really thought that the ark was much too crowded for them to visit it. So they said no thank you again quite firmly, and then ran down the river-path as fast as they could.

All the animals looked after them, and for a long time they made such a noise that John and Betty couldn't hear anything else. Soon they came to a little hill, and ran up the winding path to the top. Then who should they see coming down but Jack and Jill carrying a full pail of water between them.

She tied her handkerchief right round Jack's head and he soon stopped crying. Jill thanked Betty very much, and asked her where she was going. But before Betty could answer, Jack gave a yell.

'Look! There's the Old Woman Who Lives in a Shoe! Look out, or she'll catch us!'

At once Jack and Jill tore down the hill, and soon disappeared. John looked round and saw the Old Woman very near to them. Betty took hold of John's hand, and very quickly the two children ran away from her again.

But alas for them! The path they took led to the river! It ended there, and there was no other way out except by going into the water. Betty and John didn't know what to do. They saw Noah's Ark away in the distance, but it was too far off to be of any help.

The Old Woman came panting after them. She took hold of their hands and held them tight.

'Why do you run away, you naughty children?' she scolded. 'I have been looking for you all morning.'

'We aren't your children,' said John.
'You must let us go.'

'*Must* indeed!' said the Old Woman.
'You are like Mary Quite Contrary.
You need to learn manners. I've
whipped her and put her to bed, the
naughty little girl. Come along with
me, and have your broth without any
bread.'

Betty began to cry, and John to struggle, but it was no use. The Old Woman was just as strong as their father was and they couldn't get away. They had to go with her.

They saw Little Tommy Tucker singing for his supper, and Tom, Tom the Piper's Son, and Little Red Riding Hood on the way, but although John called to them to come and rescue them, they didn't do anything of the sort. They just ran away as fast as their legs could carry them.

Betty was still crying.

'Oh, John! she said, 'Nursery-Rhyme Land would be lovely without the Old Woman Who Lived in a Shoe. I do wish we were back in our own playroom, don't you?'

'Yes, I do,' said John. 'But it's no use wishing.'

But it *was* some use! No sooner had the two children wished their wish than something funny happened. The houses and fields began to get smaller and smaller, the paths narrower, and the people very tiny. Only the Old Woman seemed just as big as ever. She held them by the arm, and they couldn't get away.

Smaller and smaller grew the Land of Nursery Rhyme – or was it that Betty and John grew larger and larger? They didn't know. Then suddenly it wasn't a land any more – but just a big flat stretch of wallpaper, with houses and fields, ponds, river and people

painted on it. They were in their playroom!

But the Old Woman still held their arms tightly. Had she come to their nursery with them? John and Betty turned round to tell her that if she didn't let them go they would call for their mother.

And oh dear me, what a surprise! It wasn't the Old Woman after all, but Mummy herself, smiling at them.

'Well, you've been standing looking at your wallpaper so long that I really thought you'd gone to sleep!' she said. 'Come along, my dears, it's bath-time, and the water's lovely and hot.'

'Oh Mummy, we thought you were the Old Woman Who Lived in a Shoe!' said John. 'I'm *so* glad you're not!'

'Well, where did she go to?' asked Betty, staring at Mummy in surprise. 'She was here a minute ago.'

'Oh, so you *have* been asleep, then, and dreaming too!' laughed Mummy.

'No, we haven't, Mummy,' said Betty. 'We've been to the Nursery-Rhyme

Land in the wallpaper, and we had the most exciting adventures!'

But Mummy wouldn't believe her, so Betty says that next time she goes, she will ask Mary Quite Contrary for a silver bell and a cockleshell from her garden – and then Mummy will know for certain it's all as true as true can be!

The Noisy Boy

'Goodbye, Mother!' called Lennie, and he shut the door with such a bang that his mother almost fell out of her chair.

'What a noisy boy!' said his granny, who was a quiet little person, and hated sudden noises. 'If he isn't banging doors he's whistling, and if he isn't whistling he's yelling, and if he isn't yelling he's doing something with a hammer, and if he isn't hammering he's breaking something!'

Lennie's mother smiled. 'Yes, he *is* noisy,' she said. 'He always has been. I hoped he would grow out of it when he was older, but he hasn't.'

'It doesn't seem to me that you try to make him quiet,' said Granny, taking up her knitting.

'Oh, Granny, dear – we've tried everything,' said Lennie's mother. 'I've made him come back and shut the door quietly every time he bangs it. I've made him go all the way upstairs and walk down properly when he crashes down like a hurricane, I've promised him fifty pence for every day that passes without his dreadful whistling, and...'

'Well, well, well, you've done all you can!' said Granny. 'But I do wish he could see how unpleasant such a lot of noise is for people. I wouldn't want him to grow up selfish.'

Now the very next day a most peculiar thing happened to Lennie. He took the wrong turning in the wood, and ran down a path he didn't know. He was yelling like a Red Indian at the top of his very loud voice, when suddenly someone leapt out at him from behind a tree.

'SHHHHHHH!' said the someone, in a hissing voice. 'How dare you!'

'Whatever's the matter?' said Lennie, in surprise.

'Don't you know you're in Sleepy Village?' said the someone fiercely. Lennie looked at him. He was a thin, small old man, with a pointed cap on his head, hung with bells that didn't ring.

'No, I didn't,' said Lennie. 'And I don't believe it either! Silly joke you're playing on me! This is Cuckoo Wood.'

'Yes, and Sleepy Village is in the middle of Cuckoo Wood, Mr Clever!' said the old man. 'And it's where all the tired brownies and pixies and goblins come to have a rest. And here are you,

galloping along like an elephant and yelling like a thunderstorm.'

'Sorry,' said Lennie. 'But I didn't know anything about such a place. I don't think I believe in it either! Not unless I see it.'

'Well, see it then,' said the old man. 'My name is Husher. What's yours?'

'Lennie,' said Lennie, and walked beside the old man. They came out into a clearing – and there, in front of Lennie, was a collection of little crooked houses, set round in a ring. 'I suppose you're always hushing people, aren't you? What a funny job!'

Lennie began to sing, and Husher gave him a sharp slap. 'Stop that noise! Do you want to wake everyone up?'

'Don't slap me or I'll yell my head off,' said Lennie. Husher looked solemnly at him.

'You'd better be careful not to yell in this part of the wood or your head *might* come off!' he said.

Lennie felt rather uncomfortable. They went to the first house. Husher opened the door and went in. Lennie went in too – and, as usual, he banged the door. CRASH!

On a little white bed lay a sleeping goblin. When the door banged he leapt up in fright. He glared at Lennie.

'Did you do that? For two pins I'd turn you into a worm and put you down a hole!'

'Sorry,' said Lennie, in alarm. He went out quickly – and, alas, he slammed the door again. Husher gave

him a sharp slap, and hurried him away. 'Do you *want* to be a worm in a hole?' he said. 'I must say I think you're very silly.'

Lennie began to whistle a tune. He had a very piercing whistle indeed, and nobody liked it. They were passing another cottage just then, and suddenly the window flew up and out came a pair of hard, heavy boots! One struck Lennie on the shoulder, and the other hit him on the ankle.

A furious pixie-face looked out of the open window. 'That will teach you to whistle when I'm asleep!' he said angrily. 'Noisy fellow!'

'I shall have awful bruises where those boots hit me,' said Lennie crossly.

'Serves you right,' said Husher. 'I keep *telling* you this is Sleepy Village. You act as if it was Lively Town.'

They went in through a gate. Crash! Lennie banged it behind him. Then, quite forgetting, he knocked on the door loudly with the little knocker – RAT-A-TAT-A-TAT!

'SHHHHHHHHHHH!' hissed Husher, in fright, and tried to drag him away at once. But it was too late. The door flew open and out rushed an extremely angry brownie, tripping over his long beard in his rage. He carried a large slipper in his hand and

he caught hold of Lennie and gave him such a spanking that the boy yelled in fright.

'I don't like this place,' he said to Husher. 'Show me the way home.'

'Well, really, I think you *had* better go home!' said Husher. 'You'll be shut up in a box and sent to Rubbish Town if you're not careful. You do behave badly. Look, that's the path to take – down there.'

Lennie ran to the path. On the way he passed somebody's bicycle leaning by a little wall. It had a very large and shining bell. Lennie simply couldn't help ringing it.

'Jing-a-ring-a-ring!' went the bell, sounding very loud indeed in the sleepy silence of the funny little village. Even

Lennie was startled, because it was so very loud.

He felt something hit him on the right ear. An angry goblin had come to his window and thrown a piece of coal at him. Lennie threw it back – but, alas, it smashed the window. CRASH! There was a tinkling of glass which seemed to wake up everyone in the village at once.

Out of the houses came all kinds of queer folk, some in their pyjamas, some in their bare feet. They shook their fists at Lennie.

'I'll turn you into a worm! I'll change you into a blackberry and eat you! I'll change you into a candle-flame and blow you out! I'll... I'll...'

Lennie was really scared. He ran off down the path at once, with everyone after him. It led to the part of the wood he knew. He tore down his usual path, came to the lane, ran across it, and burst open the garden door at the bottom of his own garden! His granny was sitting quietly under a tree, reading. She looked up, cross.

'Oh, Lennie! Can't you come in quietly? You made me jump.'

'They're after me, they're after me!' cried Lennie, and ran into the house. Granny looked to see who was after him, but she saw no one. The folk of Sleepy Village never came as far as this.

Lennie sat down on his bed, panting. He saw that he had left his door open, and, afraid that the Sleepy Villagers might come through it, he shut it. But, dear me, he shut it quietly. And, later on, when he went downstairs, he walked quietly down instead of rushing like a hurricane. He opened the sitting-room door quietly. He spoke to his mother quietly. He didn't whistle and he didn't shout!

'How extraordinary!' said his mother to his granny later on. 'What's come over Lennie? He's not noisy any more. Do you think he's ill?'

'No, certainly not,' said Granny. 'Something happened to him this after-

noon. I don't know what. He came rushing into the garden, shouting that somebody was after him. Maybe he offended a farmer or something, and he was chasing the boy to give him a spanking. We'll ask him.'

So they did. At first Lennie wouldn't tell them about his adventure – and when he did neither his mother nor his granny believed him!

'All right!' said Lennie, offended. 'I'll soon show you it's true. I'll take you to Sleepy Village tomorrow afternoon.'

So they set off together. They took the path that led to Sleepy Village – but there was no Husher to be seen. And would you believe it, when they got to where the ring of houses had stood the day before there was only a very big ring of toadstools!

'Blow!' cried Lennie, and he stamped his foot. 'They've GONE!'

'SHHHHHHHH!' said the wind in the trees, and Lennie thought it was Husher. He ran back home then, as fast as he could, leaving Mother and Granny to come after him. And, really, you wouldn't know that noisy boy now. He's as quiet as you!

113

Jinky and the Animals

Jinky was a little fairy who didn't always want to live in Fairyland. He wanted to come to our land and know the creatures there.

He had left Fairyland once and gone to live with our birds.

'It is time I left Fairyland again,' he said to himself. 'I want to go and live with some of the animals I saw down in the world of boys and girls.

'There was a prickly creature I met one day–and a little furry thing with a long tail. And a pretty animal that bounded up the trees and down. I will go and see them all.'

So down into our world flew Jinky. First of all he went to see his old friends the robins. They were so pleased to see

him and flew down from the trees.

'Are you going to live with us again?' they said.

'No,' said Jinky. 'This time I want to live with the animals. Who do you think would be nice to me?'

'Well, whatever you do, don't go with the fierce rat,' said the robins. 'He is cruel and bad. Find a little mouse. He will be the right size for you, and maybe he will let you live with him down his hole. Look! There is a mouse in our hedgerow.'

So they called the mouse, and he came out of his hole. His little nose twitched as he looked at the fairy.

'Whiskers, this is Jinky, a friend of ours,' said the cock-robin. 'He wants to know all about animals. Will you take him with you, and tell him what you know? He would like to live with you.'

Jinky liked Whiskers. He liked his little woffly nose, his soft furry coat, and his long tail. He stroked the little mouse and Whiskers liked him.

'Yes, I'll let him live with me,' he said. 'We will have some fun. Have you warned him about the fierce rat?'

'Oh yes,' said the robins. 'Of course. And you had better warn him about the weasel and the stoat too, because they catch and eat mice, and might eat him as well!'

'Come to my hole,' said the mouse. 'I will show you where I live.'

Jinky went down the hole with the mouse. He had a cosy little room among the roots below, lined with dried grass and a little moss. 'It's cosy here,' he said. 'I hope it isn't too smelly for you.'

'Well, it *is* a bit smelly,' said Jinky, 'but I expect I shall get used to it. What are all

these shells?'

'Those? They are nut-shells,' said the mouse. 'It's hard to get food in the winter, you know, but if I have a few nuts or acorns about, I can always gnaw through the shells and have a good feast on the nut inside.'

'I like nuts too,' said Jinky, and he nibbled a bit of one. The mouse talked to him as he ate.

'I'm a small creature,' he said, 'but there are many much bigger than I am—the rabbit, for instance. He won't hurt you, because he is kind and gentle, and eats grass. The hare won't hurt you either. He lives in the open field, but the rabbit lives underground in a maze of burrows.'

'Oh, I'd like to see those,' said Jinky, at once. 'I like tunnels.'

'Well, I've a friend called Bobtail, and I'll get him to show you round,' said Whiskers. 'Then there's old Prickles the hedgehog. You'll like him. He eats beetles and slugs and things like that.

He's fond of good toadstools too. But
don't go too close to him.'

'No, I won't. I've noticed how prickly
he is,' said Jinky. 'I don't want to be
stabbed in a dozen places!'

'I'll take you to see Bushy-Tail the
squirrel, too,' said Whiskers. 'He lives up
the trees, and I only see him when he
comes to the ground. He's not very
pleased with me at present, because I
took some of the nuts he hid away for the
winter. But I didn't know they were *his*
nuts!'

'Oh,' said Jinky. 'Well, of course, you
shouldn't take his nuts. Who else do you
know?'

'There's Hopper the frog and Crawler
the toad,' said Whiskers. 'They're nice

friendly creatures. And what about Slider the snake? I'm always a bit afraid he might eat me, but I don't expect he'd eat *you*.'

'And there's Red-One the fox, and the weasel and the stoat!' said Jinky. 'But they might eat us. So we won't go too close, Whiskers! Come along, let's go and find Bobtail.'

Bobtail Makes Friends

Bobtail the rabbit was playing with many other rabbits on the side of a hill, when Whiskers took Jinky to see him.

As soon as the rabbits saw Jinky, they were afraid. They weren't used to fairies. An old rabbit thumped with his hind paws on the ground: Drm, drm, drrrrm!

'Oh dear–that's a signal for all the rabbits to run to their holes!' said Whiskers. 'Look at them!'

Jinky saw the rabbits running, their white bobtails flashing up and down as they ran. Soon they had all gone.

'Bobtail!' squealed Whiskers, going to a burrow. 'Don't be frightened. This is a friend of mine. Do come up.'

A rabbit put his head out of the burrow. Jinky put out his hand and touched the long soft ears.

'Oh, you are lovely!' he said. 'Bobtail, be friends with me. I'm only a fairy. Come out and let me see you.'

The rabbit came right out of his burrow and sniffed at Jinky. His nose woffled about like Whiskers' nose. 'You've got wings!' he said. 'But you're not a bird.'

'And you've got the longest ears I ever saw, and the shortest tail!' said Jinky. 'And the softest fur!'

The rabbit laughed. 'See my hindlegs, how long and strong they are?' he said. 'I can run fast with those. I have strong paws to dig with, too. I help to make the burrows in this hill.'

'Could I go down your burrow?' asked Jinky, feeling really excited. 'Oh, *do* take me!'

'All right,' said Bobtail, and he turned himself round to go down. 'Coming, Whiskers?'

'I'll wait here,' said the mouse. So Jinky went with Bobtail down a dark, narrow tunnel. 'Bobtail!' he called. 'What do you do with your long ears? Don't they bump into the roof?'

'Oh no!' said Bobtail. 'They're very bendable. Look, I just bend them over my back and hold them like that. Isn't this a long tunnel? And look, that one goes to the other side of the hill–and this one goes back to the hillside we've just left. And this one . . .'

'Goodness me, I should get lost at once, if you left me!' cried Jinky. 'Can I hold on to your tail in case you go too fast and leave me behind, Bobtail?'

They went on down another dark tunnel, with Jinky holding on to Bobtail.

'Bobtail, what do you do if you meet another rabbit?' called Jinky. 'You would never get by.'

'Oh, haven't you noticed the passing-places?' said Bobtail 'We're just coming to one now. I can hear another rabbit coming, so we'll wait here till he goes by.'

They came to where the tunnel widened out a little, and almost at once Bobtail heard the feet of another rabbit. At the passing-place there was just room for him to get by!

'It's a good idea to have passing-places,' said Jinky. 'I say, Bobtail, I'm tired of dark burrows now. I'm longing for the sunshine again. Could you possibly take me all the way back to where we left Whiskers?'

'Easy!' said Bobtail. 'And, if you like, I'll take you to call on Long-Ears the hare. He's my cousin, and he lives in the fields. This way–hold on to my tail!'

Down another burrow they went, and then upwards. Suddenly Jinky saw daylight, and there they were, out in the air again, just by Whiskers!

Then Bobtail took them to the field at the bottom of the hill, and called to Long-Ears the hare. He came galloping up at top speed. He had very large ears, black at the tips, and he had longer, stronger legs than Bobtail.

'Good-day!' he said. 'I've never seen a fairy before.'

'I've just taken him down to my home,' said Bobtail. 'I don't think he liked it much. You take him to see yours, Long-Ears.'

But Jinky didn't like Long-Ears' home much either. It was just a dent in the ground in the very middle of a field!

'I don't call that much of a home!' said Jinky. 'Why, it's open to the wind and the rain, and isn't at all comfortable! I'd much rather have Whiskers' home! And what do you do when enemies come,

Long-Ears? You are not very well hidden here.'

'I'll show you what I do!' said Long-Ears. He suddenly left them and ran down the field. He ran like the wind! Jinky had never seen anyone run so fast! It made him feel quite tired.

'Let's go back to your cosy hole and rest,' he said to Whiskers. 'I like your home best of all!'

Funny Little Folk

Jinky had a good rest that night, cuddled up against Whiskers' warm fur. He nibbled another nut and enjoyed it. By the time the morning came, he wanted to go and see some more of Whiskers' friends. 'What about Bushy-Tail the squirrel?' he said.

'All right,' said Whiskers, 'but remember, I told you he may be cross with me.' They left the hole and went into the wood.

'There he is, look – sitting up in that tree!' he said. 'Fly up and speak to him.'

So up flew Jinky and sat beside the bright-eyed, bushy-tailed squirrel.

He was a pretty creature. He sat up on his hind legs, and nibbled an acorn which he held in his front paws.

'Hello!' he said in surprise. 'I've not seen a fairy before. Would you like to come and live with me? I've got a fine hole in this tree!'

The hole was big and well lined. 'I sleep here in the cold winter days,' said Bushy-Tail. 'It's cosy. I wrap my big tail round me like a blanket.'

'Yes, it would make a very good blanket,' said Jinky. 'I'd like a tail like that.'

'Before I go to sleep, I'm very clever,' said the squirrel. 'Do you know what I do? Well, I know I shall wake up hungry, so I pick a lot of nuts and acorns and I hide them so that when I wake up I can have a feast!'

'Yes, I know. Whiskers told me,' said Jinky. At once Bushy-Tail got angry.

'What! Are you a friend of that little robber of a mouse?' he said. 'I'll smack you if you are!'

But Jinky didn't wait to be smacked! He flew up into the air laughing, and

landed down on the ground beside
Whiskers.

'Let's go and see someone else,' he
said. 'What about Prickles the hedgehog?'

'He's wandering about somewhere I
expect,' said Whiskers. He called to a
passing mouse, 'Hi! Have you seen
Prickles?'

'He's fast asleep in the ditch yonder,'
called the mouse. So Jinky and Whiskers
went over to the ditch. A curious little
noise came from it.

Just as Jack and Jill came up to them, Jill tripped on a stone and over she went, dragging Jack with her. The pail spilt all its water, and Jack began to howl.

'Oh dear, I *thought* you'd fall over!' said Betty. 'You always do in our picture books. Never mind, get up and I'll bind your forehead with a nice clean handkerchief.'

'It's Prickles. He's snoring,' said Whiskers. 'He often does when he's asleep. I think it's because he rolls himself up so tightly and sticks his nose into his paws.'

They came to a pile of last year's leaves. Under them was Prickles, fast asleep, curled into a prickly ball. He awoke when Whiskers squealed to him. He slowly uncurled his prickly body and stared at Jinky.

'Oh–you're nice!' said Jinky. 'I like your funny little snout, and your bright eyes, and your short little legs. Run, hedgehog, and let me see how quickly you can go!'

The hedgehog ran. He went along as if by clockwork. Jinky laughed to see him. The hedgehog came back and went a little too close to Jinky.

'Oh–you've pricked me with your spines!' cried Jinky. 'Why do you wear so many?'

'So that I can't be eaten, of course,' said the hedgehog. 'Who wants to eat a mouthful of prickles?'

He went off at a great pace. Then out of the hedge came a long, silent creature–so long that Jinky thought he was never going to end!

'It's Slider the snake,' said Whiskers, getting behind a bush. 'He's harmless, because he hasn't any poison in his bite. He's only a grass-snake. But I'm always afraid he might like me for his dinner.'

'You do get along marvellously!' said Jinky to Slider. 'You have no feet and yet you slide along as fast as I can walk. Where do you live?'

'I like to bask in the sun on the common,' said the snake. 'But I'm hungry now, so I'm going to the pond to see if I can find a frog. I shall swim after one and catch him!'

'Goodness, can you swim?' cried Jinky, looking at the snake's scaly body. It was beautifully marked, and there was a bright orange patch on his head.

'Of course,' said the snake. 'I like the water. Would you like to come with me? You needn't be afraid that I have a poisonous bite, because I haven't. My cousin the adder has, so beware of him. He may bite and he has poison at the roots of his teeth. Come along with me. You'll be quite safe.'

'No, thank you,' said Jinky. 'We might meet your cousin the adder. I think I'll go with Whiskers!' So off he went home with Whiskers again, pleased to have met so many different little animals.

The Cold Days Come

Jinky had a lovely time all that spring and summer. He met all the animals of the countryside. He liked the frog and the toad very much.

'You look rather alike,' he said, when he met them. But the frog laughed. 'Use your eyes,' he said. 'See my greeny body, so moist and soft. See my long hindlegs that take me high into the air–like this!'

He suddenly jumped very high, and startled Jinky. He landed beside him again.

'Now look at my cousin the toad's body,' he said. 'See how dry and pimply his skin is–and see how slowly he crawls. He can't hop as I can. He's a slow old thing–aren't you, Crawler?'

The toad opened his beautiful coppery eyes. 'I'm slow,' he said. 'But I'm not afraid of my enemies. See how like a clod of earth I am when I lie flat and still.'

It was quite true. He looked exactly like a clod of earth, and not a bit like a toad. 'And if enemies see me and take a bite,' he said, 'I pour out a horrible-tasting juice from my back, and nobody takes a second bite!'

'*I* escape my enemies by jumping high,' said the frog, and jumped high again. He sat down by Jinky. A big bluebottle buzzed by and, before Jinky could wave it away, the frog shot out a long tongue, caught the fly on the end of it, swallowed and blinked–and the fly was gone!

'Goodness! How did you do that?' cried Jinky. '*I* couldn't catch a fly like that with my tongue.'

'You could if you had one like mine or the toad's,' said Hopper. 'Look, it's fastened to the front of my mouth, not the back, and it's sticky! I just fling it out–like that–and catch the fly.'

'You nearly caught my nose then,' said Jinky. 'You're rather rude. Come along, Whiskers, let's go.'

Jinky saw the fierce rat, and hid from him. He looked like a great big mouse, and he had sharp teeth and a long bare tail. Jinky felt afraid of him.

He saw the weasel and the stoat, wily little animals, so good at hunting others that everyone but the fox was afraid of them. Jinky saw the red fox too, old Red-One, looking like a beautiful red-coated dog with a bushy tail.

All the rabbits fled away at the sight of him. Jinky hid too. He thought that if foxes liked rabbits they might like to eat fairies as well.

He made a great many friends, the rabbit and the hare, the squirrel, the toad and the frog. He liked all the mice, especially a little, fat, sleepy fellow called a dormouse. He liked Slider the snake too, but he hid away from the adder.

The Cold Days Come

Then the cold days came. Whiskers curled up in his hole and tried to keep warm. Prickles took some dead leaves to his hole in a warm bank, lined it well, curled up and fell fast asleep.

The toad found a big old stone with a little hiding-place under it. He crawled in there and fell asleep too. The frog hopped to the pond, leapt in, and swam to the mud at the bottom. He hid himself there and slept.

Slider the snake and his cousin the adder found an old hollow tree. They called their brothers and sisters, and all coiled together for warmth. They slept soundly too.

Jinky couldn't find many people to play with. Even Bushy-Tail the squirrel went to sleep in his hole one very cold day, and wouldn't come out to play.

The rat was hungry and fierce. The stoat and the weasel hunted all day long. The red fox was about. Jinky didn't like having to hide so often. He wondered if he should fly up to the squirrel's tree and cuddle in with him.

No, I won't, he thought. I know I shouldn't be able to sleep day after day, day after day, with no food at all, as so many of my friends are doing now. I should be bored and hungry. I'm afraid of being caught by the rat or the fox, too. I'd better go back to Fairyland for the winter.

So he went to say goodbye to Whiskers, who was nibbling a nut he had stolen from Bushy-Tail's hoard again. Bad little Whiskers!

'Goodbye, Whiskers,' said Jinky. 'I'm going back home for the winter. But I shall be here again in the spring. Don't forget me, will you?'

'Of course not,' said Whiskers. 'Will you come and live with me again?'

'No, I don't think so,' said Jinky. 'I've lived with the birds and the animals–and next time I'd like to live with the flowers and learn some of *their* secrets. But I'll come and see you, Whiskers, truly I will!'

Off he flew, back to Fairyland, and Whiskers gave his nut another nibble and then settled down to sleep.

I'll see Jinky next year, he thought. And so he will, there's no doubt about that! We'll look out for him too, won't we?

The Parcel in the Gutter

One day Sarah and James were going home from a long walk when they suddenly saw something lying in the gutter.

'What's that?' said James, surprised. 'It looks like a parcel.'

'It *is* a parcel!' said Sarah. 'How strange! Who dropped it, do you suppose?'

James picked it up. It felt rather an interesting parcel, full of knobs and bumps. He looked to see if it had a name and address.

But it hadn't. It was tied up firmly with string, and had stamps on it which had been post-marked by the post office. But there was no address on it at all.

'I know what's happened!' said Sarah. 'The postman must have come along with his van full of parcels, and one of them dropped out. And I expect the address was on a tied-on label, and it's come off.'

'What shall we do with it?' said James, feeling the bumps inside. 'It does feel an exciting parcel.'

'Let's open it,' said Sarah feeling naughty.

'Do you think we'd better?' said James. 'It doesn't belong to us.'

'Well, who *does* it belong to then?' said Sarah. 'Nobody! And I don't expect anyone will ever find out who owns it–it's got no address on at all.'

'All the same–I don't think Mummy would like us to open something that wasn't ours,' said James.

Sarah looked at him. She knew he was right. 'Well–we'd better not then,' she said. 'But what shall we do with it?'

'Take it to the post office and tell them we found it in the gutter,' said James. 'That's really the only thing to do.'

'Oh, don't let's do that, ' said Sarah.
'The post office is such a long way away
and I'm tired. Let's drop it back into the
gutter.'

'And let somebody else find it and
open it and keep the things inside!' cried
James, beginning to be cross with Sarah.
'Somebody dishonest might find it. No,
Sarah–it's to go back to the post office,
unopened–and I shall take it back
myself. You needn't come.'

'I'll come,' said Sarah, who didn't like
her brother doing anything she didn't do
too. 'I didn't mean all I said. I'm not really
as horrid as that.'

'I hope you're not!' said James, tucking the parcel under his arm. 'Come on. If we hurry we'll get there before dark.'

They hurried. They got to the post office at last, tired out, because it really was a long way away. James put the parcel down on the counter there.

'Please,' he said, 'we found this lying in the gutter. The postman must have dropped out of his van. Who do you suppose it belongs to? There's no address on it.'

The postmaster was called. He came and looked at the parcel, saw there was no address, and called to a man nearby, 'Hey, Jack! You went out with the parcels today. Have you got a loose label in the van, I wonder? These children have just brought a parcel along, without an address.'

'I'll go and look,' said the man and off he went. He soon came back. He carried a little red label with him.

'This must belong to the parcel,' he said. 'It was lying on the floor of the van. I expect it was so loosely tied on that it fell off. Don't know how I managed to drop the parcel, though. Very careless of me.'

'Yes. It's a good thing these children brought it along,' said the post master and he beamed at them. 'Nice honest children! Now let's see who the parcel is addressed to.'

He read out the label: 'Mrs Johnson, Cherry-Tree Cottage, Long Lane, Thelham.'

The children listened as if they

couldn't believe their ears. James cried out in astonishment.

'But that's our mother's name, Mrs Johnson! And that's where we live, Cherry-Tree Cottage, Long Lane!'

'Well, what a strange thing!' said the postmaster. 'You've picked up your own parcel! Good thing you didn't leave it for somebody else to pick up and open— that's what a dishonest person would have done! Then your mother would never have got her parcel!'

Sarah went very red, and James felt glad that he had done the right thing and brought the parcel to the post office, unopened.

'Shall I take it home for Mummy?' he asked. 'We're going home now.'

'Right,' said the postmaster. 'You can take it.'

So off went the two children with the parcel. Sarah spoke to James in a very small voice. 'I nearly did something very wrong, didn't I?' she said. 'I'm sorry, James.'

'It's all right,' said James. 'I wonder what's in the parcel. That looked like Granny's writing on the label. Perhaps it's a birthday present for Mummy. It's her birthday the day after tomorrow.'

Well, it *was* a birthday present for Mother, from Granny! It was a pair of fur gloves, very soft and warm. And packed with them were two other things. A tin of crayons for Sarah and a book for James!

'You picked up your own parcel and took care of it!' said Mother, when she had opened it and taken out the lovely things. 'You deserve your book, James–and you your crayons, Sarah. I might have lost these beautiful gloves, and you might not have had your book and your crayons if you hadn't done the right thing. I really feel quite proud of you!'

Sarah went red again, and James beamed all over his face. He squeezed Sarah's hand. 'Never mind!' he whispered. 'You weren't really naughty. You only wanted to be. Cheer up, and let's go and read my book.

The Bold, Bad Brownie

There was once a bold, bad brownie, who lived in the pretty village of Humble-Dumble, just outside the palace of the Lord High Chamberlain of Fairyland. His name was Tuppy, and he really was the naughtiest brownie that had ever been born.

But the funny thing was that nobody knew he was bad. Everyone thought he was very good and proper, and if he asked people to tea, they were very pleased and proud to go.

Tuppy pretended he was very, very good. He didn't tell anyone about his wicked pranks at all. Only one person knew and that was Scallywag, his big black cat, who was just as mischievous as his master.

The Bold, Bad Brownie

Scallywag kept Tuppy's cottage clean, and cooked for him. He also went with him at night when Tuppy played his naughty pranks, and kept guard for him, in case anyone came along.

I couldn't tell you all the bad things that Tuppy did. It was he who climbed up on to the roofs of the cottages and poured water down the chimneys, so that the fires below spluttered and spat, and all the village folk were frightened to death, because they thought it was a witch trying to get down the chimney.

It was Tuppy who popped glue into the high boots of the prince of Hey-ho-land, when he came to visit the chamberlain! He had seen them standing outside the gardener's shed, waiting to be cleaned, and he had poured half a pot of very sticky glue into each.

Wasn't there a scene the next day! The prince walked about in the gluey boots all day long, and didn't guess why they felt so funny – but when he came to take them off at night, he soon knew why! The glue had soaked through his stockings, and stuck to his feet, and there was no way he could get those boots off!

Well, the chamberlain made up his mind that he must find out who had done this terrible thing. So he questioned everyone, Tuppy, too, but nobody could tell him anything.

'I wonder who the wicked person is who keeps doing these dreadful things,' said Tuppy, pretending to be very upset. 'Hi! Scallywag, come here! Did you see anyone last night, when you were looking for mice?'

'Oh, yes, Master,' said Scallywag, twitching his big ears. 'I saw a witch on a broomstick. Perhaps it was she who played such a wicked trick.'

'Oho!' said the chamberlain, not dreaming that the cat was not telling the truth. 'That witch is the one who's to blame, there's no doubt.'

Tuppy enjoyed himself very much. He heard everyone talking about his last naughty prank, and he loved to listen, especially as nobody knew that

it was he, the good little Tuppy, who was to blame.

'I wish I could do something to the old chamberlain, Scallywag,' said the brownie one night. 'Wouldn't it be fun to give him a fright!'

'Ooh, yes, wouldn't it!' said Scallywag. 'Let's think of something.'

So they thought and thought, and at last Tuppy gave a shout and danced round the room.

'I know, I know!' he cried. 'I'll dress up as a witch, and climb up to the chamberlain's bedroom tonight. I'll wake him up, and pretend to put him under a fearful spell. He'll think I really am a witch, and he'll be dreadfully frightened. I'll make him give me a bag of gold, and then we shall be very rich indeed, and needn't work any more.'

'That's a fine idea,' said Scallywag. 'I'll go out and borrow you some witch's clothes.'

So out went the wicked cat, and after roaming round the countryside for some time, came to a little cottage set on a hill. Witch Nimble lived there, and Scallywag soon crept in at the window, and went to the cupboard where she kept her best clothes. He took a black cloak, and a pointed hat. Then back he went to Tuppy, who was delighted.

'I'll go tonight to the palace,' he chuckled. 'Help me on with these things, Scallywag. My! I shall look fine.'

He did too, just exactly like a witch,

with his black cloak flowing out round him, and his pointed hat pulled well down over his forehead.

Tuppy could hardly wait for the night to come. As soon as he heard the village clock strike twelve, he set out with Scallywag to the palace. He found it quite easy to get into the garden, and then he went to the window which he knew belonged to the chamberlain's bedroom.

Up he went, Scallywag helping him. Soon he stood up in the bedroom, trying to find out where the chamberlain's bed was.

Then he saw it, and made his way over to it. There was a tiny night-light burning, and Tuppy saw that the chamberlain was lying on his side, with his face turned away from him.

He tiptoed across to the bed, and then, seeing a large sponge in a basin of water, he picked it up, and squeezed it over the chamberlain's head. The chamberlain spluttered and choked and, was just going to turn round and

sit up when Tuppy spoke, in a very deep voice.

'Do not move, Sir Chamberlain. I am a witch, very powerful and strong. I shall put a spell on you, unless you do what I wish.'

'What do you want?' asked the chamberlain, in a frightened voice.

'I want a bag of gold,' said Tuppy.

'Well, the key of the treasure-chest is hanging on the wall just by you,' said the chamberlain. 'Take what you want and g-g-go.'

Tuppy thought his plan was going beautifully. He looked for the key but couldn't see it.

'Whereabouts did you say the key was?' he asked the chamberlain.

'Hanging on the wall just b-b-b-by you,' answered the chamberlain, still not turning round.

Tuppy looked again, but he couldn't see it anywhere.

'There's no key here,' he said.

'Yes, look, there it is,' said the chamberlain, suddenly turning round and pointing. Tuppy was taken off his guard, and looked to see where the chamberlain was pointing: and that was just what the chamberlain wanted! He hadn't been a bit frightened, really, but had just been waiting for a chance to turn round safely.

In a flash his out-stretched hand darted at Tuppy's shoulder. Tuppy dodged – and then, alas for the brownie, the chamberlain's hand caught firmly hold of Tuppy's nose and held tight!

'Ow! Oh! Ooh! Let go!' cried Tuppy. But the chamberlain wouldn't. Tuppy had rather a long nose, anyhow, and as perhaps you know, brownies' noses are very easy to pull out of shape. Tuppy's nose began to get longer and longer as the chamberlain pulled at it!

When it was about a metre long, the chamberlain felt twenty sharp needles running into his right leg. He let go of Tuppy's nose with a howl, and the brownie at once ran to the window and leapt out. Scallywag, who had come to his master's rescue by digging all his claws into the poor chamberlain, sprang out after him, and the two raced through the garden and out into the road. In three minutes they were safely at home.

Then Scallywag saw Tuppy's nose.

'Ooh, Tuppy!' he said. 'What are you going to do about your nose? The chamberlain will send his soldiers out tomorrow to find someone with a long nose, and you can't hide it, you know.'

Tuppy began to cry, and Scallywag was very upset.

'I know!' he said at last. 'I'll go to old Mother Jum-Jum, who lives at the other end of the village. She is very good with noses, because when Pixie

Twiddle had his nose stung by a wasp, so that it swelled out terribly, she put a spell on it and it went back to its right size at once.'

'Yes, but she'll tell the soldiers that she mended my nose, and they'll know all about me, then,' wept Tuppy.

'I'll blindfold her, and lead her here with all sorts of twists and turns,' said Scallywag. So off he went. Mother Jum-Jum said she would mend anyone's nose; she didn't want to know whose it was, so Scallywag blindfolded her, and led her to Tuppy's through all sorts of twists and turns. She put a spell on his long nose, and in a trice it went back to its proper size again. Then Scallywag led Mother Jum-Jum back to her neat cottage.

Well, the soldiers went out the next morning to find someone with a long nose, but of course they couldn't find anyone at all. But they did find that Mother Jum-Jum had mended someone's nose, though she couldn't say whose nor could she say where he lived, because she had been taken there blindfolded.

'Perhaps if you blindfolded me again I could lead you,' she said to the captain of the soldiers. 'I believe I could remember all the turns and twists that I took.'

So she was blindfolded, and led the way quite correctly to Tuppy's house that night. The captain took out a piece of chalk, and marked a white cross on the door, meaning to go and get his soldiers, and arrest whoever lived in that cottage.

But it so happened that Scallywag, coming home from his nightly hunt, saw the cross, and at once guessed what it was for. In a trice he took a piece of chalk and marked every house in the village just the same!

When the captain came into the streets the next morning with his soldiers, he was amazed to find that every single house was marked with white crosses. So, of course, it was quite impossible for him to tell which one he wanted.

That night he made Mother Jum-Jum lead him to Tuppy's once more. This time he chipped a piece off the doorstep, and then off he went to tell his soldiers that he had found the right house again.

But Scallywag, now on the look out, saw the chipped doorstep, and taking a hammer, he went to every other door-step in the village and carefully chipped a piece out. He wasn't going to have his master discovered, not he!

The captain was very angry when he

found what had happened. Doorstep after doorstep he found chipped, and he knew that it was no good looking for the house he had marked.

'But I'll beat the scoundrel this time, whoever he is!' he said. So that night, when Mother Jum-Jum had led him to Tuppy's again, he climbed up to the roof and tied a red ribbon round the chimney pot. On it he put a fly-away spell, so that at dawn it would untie itself and fly right away.

Scallywag soon saw the ribbon when he came home from his hunting. He couldn't very well help seeing it, for it stood out against the bright moon. Scallywag ran to the draper's, jumped in at the window, and took all the red ribbon there was. Then out he went and tied a piece to the chimney of every house in the village. How funny they looked! But Scallywag didn't think of that. He was glad that he had once more saved his master.

He told Tuppy what he had done, and that bad brownie chuckled long and loud. Then they both curled up together and slept soundly. They didn't hear the fly-away spell make a whistling noise at dawn, or see the ribbon untie itself and fly away. They heard nothing at all. They would have been terribly upset if they had known that theirs was the only house in the village without a ribbon round the chimney-pot.

The captain came marching through at sunrise, his keen eyes looking at every chimney. He saw one after

164

another decorated gaily with red ribbon – and then he came to Tuppy's. That had no ribbon on, and at once the captain knew that this was the house to whose chimney he had tied a ribbon with a fly-away spell on it.

'Surround the house!' he cried. 'A witch lives here, the one who has been playing such wicked tricks for years. Be careful!'

The soldiers surrounded the house. The captain walked up to the front door, and knocked very loudly. Tuppy peeped out of the window, and saw the soldiers. How frightened he was, and how upset Scallywag was!

There was nothing to do but to open the door. When the captain saw Tuppy he was very much astonished.

'Tuppy!' he cried. 'You don't mean to say it was you who pretended to be the witch, and did such wicked things! Oh, Tuppy, and we thought you were such a good brownie!'

Then Tuppy began to cry bitterly, but it wasn't any good. He was taken off

by the soldiers, and brought in front of the angry chamberlain.

'You, Tuppy!' cried the chamberlain in a fury. 'Oh! Take him away, captain, and spank him hard. Spank him very hard indeed, and then put him into prison until he promises to be good. As for Scallywag, the cat, spank him too, and shut him up in the cellar!'

So Tuppy was spanked hard, and taken to prison, where he had to stay until he promised faithfully to be good. But no one knows where Scallywag is. As soon as he heard he was to be spanked, he gave a loud miaow, and leapt straight up the chimney; and nobody has ever heard of him since.

The Little Button Elves

One-Button, Two-Button, Three-Button, Four-Button and Five-Button were five little elves who were so alike that no one could tell which was which.

Because of this, one of them wore only one button on his tunic, the next had two buttons, and so on – and everyone called them by the number of their buttons.

'Here comes One-Button!' the pixie-folk used to cry as they saw the elf with one button coming down the road.

'Two-Button is out shopping,' they said when they saw the elf with two buttons going out with a basket. It was quite easy to tell which was which by counting the buttons.

Now one day all five elves went out

together to picnic on Bumblebee Common. One-Button carried the kettle, Two-Button carried the bread and butter, Three-Button carried the cakes, Four-Button carried the apples and Five-Button carried the cups and plates.

Just as they were crossing over the little bridge that leads to the common, Three-Button stumbled and fell. He only just managed not to fall into the water beneath – but alas, the cakes did!

How upset all the Button-Elves were! It was dreadful to have no cakes at a picnic tea. Three-Button was very sorry about it, but it couldn't be helped.

They found a nice place to have their picnic and then Three-Button said that, as he had lost the cakes, he would take the job of going to ask for water for their kettle. So off he started. He saw a cottage in the distance and walked towards it. As he drew near to it, he smelt a delicious smell of newly made cakes.

He knocked on the door and an old

dame opened it.

Three-Button thought that she looked very like a witch, but she had kind eyes so he felt sure that she couldn't be.

'Please may I have some water for my kettle?' he asked. 'Certainly,' said the old dame. 'Step into my kitchen and take some from the tap.'

So Three-Button walked into the kitchen and filled his kettle.

Then he suddenly caught sight of the table and his eyes and mouth opened in surprise – for it was piled high with hundreds of cakes, all newly-made and smelling simply delicious!

Three-Button remembered how he had dropped the picnic cakes into the water and a very naughty thought came into his head. Surely the old dame would never miss five cakes from such a big pile.

In a trice the naughty little elf snatched five buns from the table, took up his kettle, and ran out of the door.

He raced back to the others and showed them what he had got – but he didn't tell them that he had stolen the buns.

They were very pleased.

Soon the kettle was boiling away merrily and One-Button made the tea. Then the elves set to work on the bread and butter. When they had finished that, they started on the newly-baked cakes. They were simply delicious!

But just as they were handing one another the apples, a curious thing happened. Each elf began to feel very uncomfortable.

They looked at one another and then cried out in dismay. 'We're all getting very fat!' they cried, and pointed to each other.

Sure enough they were! Their little tunics became very tight, and their toes burst out of their boots. Soon their hats were much too small and fell off their heads.

'What is it?' cried One-Button. 'What can be the matter with us?'

But none of them knew. It was really dreadful. They grew bigger and bigger and at last, with a pop, One-Button's little button flew off his tunic! Then Two-Button's two buttons flew off too, and Three-Button's and Four-Button's.

Five-Button's popped off as well and soon the grass was strewn with all their buttons.

Crying bitterly they ran home. Everyone they met stared at them in astonishment. When they got home, they shut themselves up and looked all through their magic books to find out what was the matter with them.

And very soon they discovered that

pimpernel cakes eaten newly-made caused people to grow terribly fat all in a hurry.

Then Three-Button began to sob and he confessed to the others that he had stolen the five cakes he had brought to them. 'I expect they must have been pimpernel cakes,' he wept. 'I remember seeing a lot of pimpernels growing round the old woman's cottage. Oh, whatever are we to do?'

'Wait a minute!' cried One-Button eagerly. 'Here is a page that tells us what to do to get back to our own size again. Listen: Melt salt and sugar together in a silver thimble and drink it in front of a fire. Then you will grow thin once more!'

It wasn't long before all the elves were solemnly drinking salt and sugar from silver thimbles in front of their kitchen fire.

No sooner had they finished than they suddenly shrank back to their ordinary size! How glad they were! They took hands and danced round and round in glee.

Just then a pixie friend of theirs came in to see them.

'Oh,' he said, 'I just wanted to know if Two-Button would — but, dear me, which of you *is* Two-Button? You haven't any buttons on at all and you're so alike that I can't possibly tell which is which!'

The Button-Elves looked at each other.

Of course, the Buttons had popped off their tunics when they had grown so fat — and now no one would know which was which! And to make things much worse, the elves themselves couldn't remember who had one button, and who had two, three, four and five.

'*Now* what are we to do?' asked the elves in despair. 'Who can tell us who is who?' All the little folk of the town came to try and help them but, really, the elves were so much alike that it wasn't a bit of use.

'There is only one person who could help you and that is Dame Pimpernel up on Bumblebee Common,' said a pixie. 'She is a very clever person indeed.'

'That must be the old woman whose cakes we took,' said one of the Button-Elves. 'Well, we'd better go and confess, and perhaps she will help us.'

So off they all went and soon arrived at Dame Pimpernel's cottage.

She was very much surprised to see

them, and even more astonished when she heard that they had stolen five of her cakes and had grown so fat.

When she heard that all their buttons had popped off, she laughed till the tears ran down her wrinkled cheeks.

'Please don't laugh at us,' begged the elves. 'We have managed to get thin again but, you see, we don't know which of us is which now. People say that you are clever and can tell us.'

'I can tell you easily enough,' said old Dame Pimpernel. 'But you must do something for me in return. You have certainly been punished for the naughtiness of one of you but I think you should be punished a little more. The next time you will all remember not to touch things belonging to other people.'

'What shall we do for you, then?' asked the Button-Elves humbly.

'You can come and feed my chickens for me every day,' said the old woman. 'I really haven't time.'

'Very well, we will take it in turns to

come every day,' promised the elves. 'Now do please tell us which is which.'

'Well, One-Button's button has gone, but his one button-hole has not!' said the dame with a laugh, and she hooked her finger into One-Button's one button-hole. 'You are One-Button. Two-Button is the one with two button-holes, of course, and Three-Button the one with three. Four-Button and Five-Button can easily find themselves by

counting *their* button-holes too. What a lot of little sillies you are! You could easily have thought of that for yourselves.'

Then the Button-Elves began to laugh. 'Ha-ha!' they went. 'He-he! Ho-ho! What sillies we are! Thank you, Dame Pimpernel; now we will go home and sew on our buttons again. Tomorrow One-Button will come and feed your chickens for you!'

Off they ran and got out their needles and thread. They sewed on their buttons and then felt very happy, for once again they knew which of them was which.

Each day they take it in turns to feed Dame Pimpernel's chickens. On baking-day they smell the newly-made cakes and see them on the kitchen table — but you may be sure that not one of the Button-Elves goes near them!

The Grumple Goblin

There was once a goblin who lived in a little crooked house called Grumple Cottage. He was a very unkind fellow who was rude to everyone. Nobody liked him, and as he was very friendly with witches and wizards, the little folk of the village were rather afraid of him.

Grumple was ugly. He had a very long nose, two long pointed ears, and tiny little eyes. The only nice things about him were his feet. They were small and dainty, and Grumple was very proud of them indeed.

The elves and pixies around used to run away when they saw Grumple coming. He liked to pull their hair and pinch their arms, and once he gave Silvertoes a cake filled with pepper that made her sneeze all day long. Another day he caught a little robin and kept it in a cage for a week, though such a thing was strictly forbidden in Fairyland. The elves came and begged

him to set the little bird free, but he only laughed at them.

'If only we could make Grumple go away from Fairyland,' sighed the pixies and elves. 'He spoils our little village. He keeps his garden in a terribly untidy state, and his weeds spread their seeds everywhere. He doesn't pay his bills, and he isn't a bit polite. If only he would go away!'

But Grumple wouldn't. He enjoyed teasing all the little folk around, and if he could do anything to annoy them, he would.

'*I'm* not going away!' he said. 'I'm going to live here all my life. You won't get rid of *me*!'

Then one day the elves and pixies held a meeting about Grumple.

'We *must* make him go away,' they said. 'He is quite spoiling our village. Let us offer a reward to anyone who will make him leave.'

'Yes,' said an elf. 'We will give ten pounds in gold coins to anyone who can do such a clever thing as that.'

Now at the meeting there was a little elfin cobbler, called Twinkle. He lived in the village and he was very poor indeed – so poor that he couldn't even afford to make himself a pair of shoes. When he heard of the reward he sat in his seat and thought hard.

If I could get those gold coins, I should be able to marry a little wife and be very happy, he thought. I should put a new roof on my old cottage, and buy a new kitchen teapot. I should get a new coat and make myself a pair of shoes. Then I should ask Goldie-wing to marry me, and we would be very happy together.

He went home and thought very hard again. For a long time he could think of no way to win the ten pounds. Then at last a splendid idea came to him and he jumped up and clapped his hands in glee.

He put on his hat again and ran out of the cottage to the house on the common where Trim the brownie lived. He knocked at the door and Trim opened it.

'Could you let me have a walking spell?' he asked.

'Well, you'll have to pay me,' said Trim. 'They are expensive, you know.'

'I can't pay you now,' said Twinkle. 'But I may have ten pounds in a few days, and I'll pay you then.'

'Good gracious!' said Trim, in surprise. 'How rich you are going to be, Twinkle!'

'I hope so,' said Twinkle. 'Please get me the spell, Trim, for I'm in a hurry.'

Trim went to his cupboard and took out a box of spells. He chose one and wrapped it up in paper. Then he gave it to Twinkle. The elf thanked him and ran off gleefully.

As soon as he got home he took a piece of blue leather and began to make

a pair of shoes. He worked all night long and soon the prettiest pair of shoes that he had ever made lay under his hands.

'Ha!' said Twinkle. 'I think you'll do, little shoes! Now, where's that spell?'

He shook the spell out of its paper, and broke it in half. Then he put one half into the toe of one shoe, and the other half into the toe of the second shoe, and pressed them down hard.

By that time it was daylight, for he had worked all night long. Twinkle put his head down on his arms and slept soundly for two hours. He woke up as the clock struck eight, and jumped from his stool as fresh as a lark.

He took the little blue shoes and put them right in the very middle of his window. Then he popped his hat on once more and ran to visit his friends.

'Listen,' he said to them. 'I have a lovely pair of blue shoes in my window. I have made them for Grumple's feet. I want you to go and tell him what a beautiful pair they are and perhaps he will come and buy them. Then you will see something funny!'

All his friends were very excited to hear this, and they promised to go and see Grumple that very morning. So one by one they wandered past his cottage. Grumple was sitting at his garden gate reading a newspaper, his feet in a pair of smart brown shoes. He stuck them out well in front of him, for he was really very proud of them.

'Good morning, Grumple,' said the first elf. 'What nice feet you have! You ought to go and look in Twinkle's window. He has the prettiest pair of shoes there that ever you saw!'

Grumple looked at his feet and admired them.

'I'm sure the cobbler hasn't such smart shoes as these brown ones in his window!' he said.

'Oh, they're *much* nicer!' said a pixie. 'They have blue laces to match, and a pretty pattern worked on the toes. They are simply lovely. But I don't think they would fit anyone but you, Grumple, because no one has such nice feet as you have.'

How pleased Grumple was to hear this! He loved people to notice his feet. It was not often that any elf or pixie spoke to him, and he was pleased that so many people should come and tell him that Twinkle had a pair of shoes that would just suit his feet.

So many elves and pixies came and told him about the blue shoes that he thought he really must go and see them for himself.

Perhaps, if they are not very expensive, I might buy them, he thought. They would go nicely with my new blue coat.

He put on his hat, took his stick under his arm and marched off to Twinkle's shop. The elf saw him coming, and shook with excitement. If only his plan would work!

Grumple stood outside the window and looked at the blue shoes.

Yes, he thought, they are lovely. They will match my new coat. I will go and buy them.

He walked into the shop. Twinkle bowed to him and asked him what he could do for him.

'Bring me those blue shoes,' said Grumple. 'How much are they?'

'Twenty pence the pair,' said Twinkle, fetching them from the window.

'*Much* too dear!' said Grumple, who was terribly mean, 'If they fit me I will pay you fourpence for them.'

'Let me try them on,' said Twinkle. 'You will see if you like them then.'

Grumple sat down on a chair and took off his brown shoes. Twinkle unlaced one of the blue shoes, and looked at Grumple's feet, hoping that the shoes would slip on easily.

'Haven't I got nice feet?' said the vain goblin. 'Don't you wish you had feet like mine?'

'These shoes will just fit you nicely,'

187

said Twinkle. He slipped one shoe on and laced it up tightly. Then he put the other one on and laced that up too.

'Yes,' said Grumple, very pleased with the look of them. 'I will have them. I will pay you tenpence for them.'

'You can pay twenty pence,' said Twinkle, firmly.

'No, tenpence,' said Grumple. 'They feel a bit funny at the toes. Tenpence is what I will pay you for them.'

'Very well,' said Twinkle. 'Pay me tenpence.'

He put down the money on the counter and then walked out of the shop. He was very proud of his new shoes, for they were certainly the prettiest he had ever had. They felt rather tight at the toes but he wasn't going to bother about that.

He was surprised to see a great many elves and pixies outside the shop. They looked at his feet and smiled at one another. Grumple thought they were admiring his feet and he stuck them out as much as he could as he walked.

the hill and watched him hurrying away in the distance, unable to stop himself.

'There he goes!' they cried in delight. 'He's so far away now that he looks like a little black dot! The walking spell will take him right out of Fairy-land, and he'll never come back again!'

Twinkle laughed in glee. He was so pleased that his plan had worked. The little folk held a meeting straight away and gave the cobbler a bag with ten pounds of golden coins inside. He was so joyful!

Off he went to Goldie-wing and told her that she was to marry him the very next week. Then he bought a new roof for his cottage, a new kitchen teapot and a new coat for himself. He made a lovely pair of red shoes for Goldie-wing and a pair of green ones for himself. He paid Trim for the walking spell, and then the day came for the wedding.

What a fine time they had! All the bluebells rang their loudest, and the

May trees gave their petals for confetti. Twinkle was the happiest little elf in the whole of Fairyland!

'I wonder where Grumple is now!' he said. 'I expect he's walked to the other end of the world! I hope I never see him again!'

Nobody knows what happened to the Grumple goblin. Perhaps he walked over the rainbow bridge to the moon!